Thank you God for our day in the town

Eira Reeves

For Charlotte, my goddaughter

Judson Press ® Valley Forge

Mommy gave Katie and Mark their spending money. "You can go shopping in town with Auntie Sue," she said.

What do you buy with your spending money?

Auntie Sue met them at the bus stop.
They took a red bus to town.

What color are your buses?

"Let's look in the toy shop window," said Katie.
There was a tractor, cars, dolls, and a teddy bear.

Which is your favorite toy?

"I'd like an apple," said Mark.
So they stopped at the greengrocer's.
With some of their spending money they
bought two juicy apples.

What other fruit can you see?

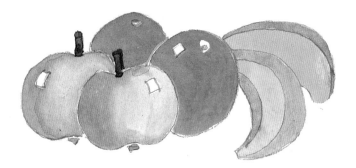

"Listen!" said Auntie Sue. "I can hear music."
Further along the street they saw a man playing a trumpet.

What noise does a trumpet make?

"We'll go to the supermarket next," said Auntie Sue.

"I'm good at pushing the cart," said Mark.

"I like filling it up," said Katie.

How do you like to help with the shopping?

"It's Mommy's birthday tomorrow. Let's buy her some chocolate," suggested Katie.

"You've picked your favorite kind!" laughed Mark.

You could paint a birthday card for a friend.

In the department store Auntie Sue
bought a sweater.
"Like my hat?" asked Katie.

How many hats can you see?

"Time for a rest in the park," said Auntie Sue.
Katie and Mark went on the swings. A friendly dog came to say hello.

What else can you do in the park?

A clown came by, handing out balloons.
"Bring all your friends to the circus
tomorrow!" he said.
"May I have a balloon for Auntie,
please?" asked Mark.

What colors are the balloons?

"Who would like an ice cream cone before we go home?" asked Auntie Sue. The ice cream man gave a strawberry cone to Mark and a chocolate cone to Katie.

What flavors of ice cream do you like?

At bedtime Katie and Mark talked to
God and said, "Thank you, God, for our
day in the town."

What did you do today? Tell God about it.

© Eira Reeves 1988   First published 1988
All rights reserved.
Published in the U.S.A. by Judson Press, P.O. Box 851, Valley Forge, PA 19482-0851
ISBN 0-8170-1136-6 U.S.A.
Worldwide co-edition organized and produced by Angus Hudson Ltd., London.
Printed in England by Purnell Book Production Limited